Mystery
of the
Troubled
Toucan

BY LISA TRAVIS

ILLUSTRATIONS BY ADAM TURNER

Published by WorldTrek Publishing

Copyright © 2015 by Pack-n-Go Girls

Printed in the USA

Visit our website at www.packngogirls.com.

This is a work of fiction. Names, characters, places, and incidents either are the product of the author's imagination or are used fictitiously. The city of Manaus, Brazil, is real, and it's a wonderful place to visit. Any other resemblance to actual events, locales, organizations, or persons, living or dead, is entirely coincidental and beyond the intent of either the author or the publisher.

Illustrations by Adam Turner

ISBN 978-1-936376-24-7

Cataloging-in-Publication Data available from the Library of Congress.

To Rich, my best friend in the adventures of our amazing family.

Contents

Meet the Characters

Sofia Diaz
always likes to have a
plan. But she didn't
think she would need
so many plans to solve
the mysteries in the
Amazon rainforest.

Júlia Santos
loves exploring the
rainforest. She wants
to become a ranger
so she can protect
the animals of the
Amazon.

Mr. Diaz

is Sofia's dad. He works for a motorcycle factory that has an office in Manaus, Brazil.

Senhor Santos

is Júlia's dad. He works with Mr. Diaz. He's excited to show Mr. Diaz and Sofia the Amazon rainforest.

The Troubled Toucan

is sending a message!
What is it?

And now, the mystery begins . . .

Mystery of the Troubled Toucan

Chapter 1

Coming Apart

Putt. Putt. Putt. Sputter. Putt. Putt. Sputter. Putt.
Sputter. Sputter. Sput—

Sofia Diaz whirled around and peered over the
side of the sputtering boat. The dark waters of the
Rio Negro slowed down as they flowed past. Her
dad had told her that the Rio Negro flowed together
with the Rio Solimões to create the Amazon River in
Manaus. Up river, where they were, she could really
see why the Rio Negro was named after the color of

the water. It meant "black river." The waters looked blacker now, even threatening, as the boat sputtered and slowed to a stop.

"Um, Dad, did the boat just die?" She wouldn't be surprised. The run-down wooden boat had blue paint peeling off the sides and a makeshift tarp duct-taped to the top for shade.

"I'm sure it's nothing Sofie-Bear," Mr. Diaz said. That was her nickname. Sofie-Bear. Her mom said that when she was born, she cried so loud all the hospital nurses were afraid of her. A bear, they agreed. She didn't mind though. She loved that her long, dark brown hair and matching dark brown eyes were just like a brown bear. Plus, bears were strong and tough, and so was she. She could clench her sturdy jaw and give a fierce growl when she wanted to. But right now she felt much less like a big, bold bear and much more like a tiny, timid mouse.

Coming Apart

Squawk! Yelp! Yelp! Yelp!

Sofia jumped. She squinted, trying to find the source of the eerie sound coming from the lush broad-leafed rainforest that lined the Rio Negro.

Squawk! She heard it again. Sofia saw a flash of black and white hopping from tree to tree as they floated on the river. A toucan. Its giant bright red, blue, and yellow beak stood out against the canopy of green. Just yesterday she had been home in Miami watching the pelicans, with their giant beaks, fly by on their hourly patrol of the beach.

Thinking of home reminded her of things she wished she could forget. Her stomach tightened. She especially wanted to forget what she'd heard her dad say on his phone last week. "I'm doing my best, but I think this just isn't working," her dad had said. "Well, then, I think I'd better find an apartment," he'd said. She ran to tell her brother, Luis, what she'd heard. But he was only seven and didn't understand anything. So then she told her fifteen-year-old brother, Aldo. His faced clouded over. He went straight to their parents that night. She followed right behind.

"Your dad and I have talked about this a lot. We think it will be better for everyone if we live in separate places," her mom had said. "It has nothing to do with you. We both love you kids so very much." Her mom was teary-eyed as she hugged them. Her dad kept running his fingers through his hair. That's what he did when he was stressed.

Sofia wasn't sure what that meant for their family, but she was sure it wouldn't be good. Where would she live? Would she see both of her parents? Would they both still love her? Would she live with her brothers?

Then before she could even come up with a plan for the rest of her life, she and her dad zipped off to Manaus, Brazil. He had a business trip for the motorcycle company that he worked for. He insisted Sofia come along.

"I'll meet with the Brazilian office managers. Afterwards, my co-worker is taking us on a trip into the Amazon rainforest. His daughter, Júlia, is your age. It'll be fun!" How could she have fun after this horrible week? Her family was coming apart. Her whole life was coming apart. Now this boat was coming apart. She sighed and wiped a tear from the corner of her eye.

Her dad was looking toward the back of the boat, running his fingers through his hair again. She followed her dad's eyes. Hugo, the captain of the boat, yanked the motor's starter rope. Nothing. He slammed the motor with his rough hand and shook his head in disgust. Then he did it again— the rope *and* the slamming. Still nothing.

"*Nada,*" Hugo muttered. Sofia frowned. She knew this meant "nothing," at least in Spanish.

This seemed to be one of those words that was similar in Portuguese.

Hugo spit in the water as he turned around. The brim of his dirty blue hat covered one eye. His other eye, so dark brown it was almost black, shifted under his furrowed brow.

"Estamos presos." We're stuck. Hugo's lip curled up in a slight grin revealing cracked yellow teeth. What was there to smile about when you were stuck on a broken boat in the middle of the Amazon?

That was just plain creepy, Sofia thought. Maybe this was his plan. To pretend the boat was broken and then steal their things. Well, now she needed a plan. She found her inner bear, took a deep breath, and pushed the rest of her thoughts aside.

"Um, Dad, can we get another boat to help us or something?"

"Well, Sofia, we're not in Miami anymore," Mr. Diaz sighed. "On the Intercoastal, there would be lots of boats to help us. Do you see any other boats here right now?"

"No, not really," Sofia said. She looked down at her hands.

Sofia stole a quick look at Hugo. He stood at the stern of the boat with his arms folded over his torn t-shirt. His black eyes stared back at her. Was he trying to figure out the best time to rob them? Or, worse yet, was he waiting for the rest of his thief friends to join him? He'd take their things, jump into a getaway boat, and leave them on this broken boat forever. Her life would come apart even more.

"Maybe we could swim to shore and get help," Sofia urged. That was a good plan. She peered over the side of the boat into the river's black water again. It was so dark she couldn't see anything under the surface. The water rippled.

"Well, we could. But there are caiman in the river here," Mr. Diaz replied.

"Caiman?" Sofia asked.

"Crocodiles. They also call them *jacaré.*"

Sofia shuddered. In Miami, she was used to alligators, not crocodiles. But she didn't want to swim with either one. She liked her legs and arms way too much.

"And there are piranhas," he added. "You know. The fish with the razor-sharp teeth."

Sofia shuddered again. She'd have nightmares for a week.

"*. . . e o sucuri,*" Hugo hissed with a crooked grin.

"And the anaconda," Mr. Diaz translated.

"Don't forget about the 300-pound, 20-foot long anacondas."

Giant snakes too? Sofia rubbed the sides of her head with her hands. Her plan was coming apart, just like her life and this rickety old boat she was stuck in.

Chapter 2

A Quick Fix?

PUTT PUTT

She needed a *new* plan. Fast. Who knew when Hugo's thief friends would get here? The wheels turned in Sofia's mind.

"Okay, Sofia. You can't swim to shore for help," she mumbled to herself. "So, that's out." She looked around the boat. Hugo pounded on the motor again, yanking the starter rope.

She moved the pieces of the puzzle around in her mind. Her grandfather, Buelo, was really good at fixing things. In fact, he even built his own wooden boat. Sometimes she would work with him in the garage. He thought girls should learn how to build and fix things. What would he do right now? Then it hit her. She knew exactly what to do. And it just might work!

Sofia hopped up and grabbed her dad's hand. She dragged him to the back of the boat.

"What's up, Sofia?"

"I think I know what's wrong," Sofia said. She looked Hugo directly in the eye and motioned for him to move away from the motor. His creepy grin grew even wider and ended with a snort. I guess he thought girls couldn't fix anything. Well, she would show him. She was a bear, not a mouse.

Sofia reached down and moved the gas line to the other tank. She had done it hundreds of times with Buelo. Well, maybe not hundreds of times, but enough to know how to switch gas tanks.

Mr. Diaz pulled the starter rope again. Nothing. He tried a second time. Still nothing.

Hugo laughed out loud.

"Well, it's not bad gas then," Sofia sighed. Beads of sweat formed under the bangs on her forehead and down her back. She was certainly used to hot, sticky weather in Miami, and the Amazon was not too different. But Hugo's snicker and glowering stare made her even more flush.

"Dad, do you remember that time we were dead in the water and the yacht was heading right toward us? Wasn't Buelo trying to fix a filter or something? Do you think it could be that?"

"Let's find out," Mr. Diaz replied as he turned off the gas and took the cover off of the motor. "Can you stick your hand in the right side of the motor over here? You see that? You need to use your fingernails to pop off the red clamps on either end of the filter."

Now Sofia added dirt and grease on top of the sweat. But she didn't care. Anything to get off this boat. She reached in and popped out the filter.

Mr. Diaz cleaned it out as best he could. Then he snapped it back in the motor. Hugo put on the cover, turned the gas on, and pulled the starter rope. Sputter . . . Sputter . . . they held their breaths.

Putt. Putt. Putt. Putt. Putt. Putt.

"It worked!" Sofia smiled wide at Hugo. He looked away.

What? No *"Obrigado,* Sofia" or "Thank you, Sofia, for your brilliant plan?" Of course, he was probably mad because she ruined his plot to rob them. She frowned, turned, and stomped to her seat under the tarp.

The boat putted up the river. But not fast enough for Sofia. All she wanted to do was get off this rickety old boat, get away from Mr. Creepy, and get back to her family. Her family. If only she could fix her family as easily as she fixed the boat. Her stomach churned. She rested her head on the side of the boat and watched the black water run slowly by. After what seemed like hours, the boat pulled up to a wooden dock lined with canoes. A small, weathered building stood on the wider part of the dock near the shore. As Sofia scrambled out of the boat, she looked back at Hugo.

"Dad, do we have to take that same boat when we leave?" She closed her eyes and prayed his answer would be "no."

"Don't worry about leaving. We just got here," Mr. Diaz replied.

Don't worry? She was worried. She hoped she would NEVER run into creepy Hugo again.

Chapter 3

The Troubled Toucan

"Bem-vinda ao Brasil!" Sofia jumped. She turned to see who owned the loud voice behind her. There stood a slight girl who looked a lot like her. She had brown eyes with brown hair that looked a little lighter and a little thicker than Sofia's. She wore it up too, but not in a tight ponytail like Sofia. Her hair was just clipped in the back, with wavy strands falling out all over. Her bright smile lit up against her light brown skin. She hopped down the wooden stairs to the dock.

"Boa tarde! Meu nome é Júlia. Prazer em conhecé-la," the girl said. Sofia looked at her blankly. "Good afternoon, my name is Júlia. Nice to meet you," she repeated in English. "Welcome to the Anavilhanas Archipelago."

"Ana-va-what?" Sofia stammered.

"Hi Júlia," Mr. Diaz stuck his hand out to greet her. "I'm Mr. Tony Diaz. And this is Sofia, who I'm afraid has forgotten her manners. Sofia, this is Senhor Santos' daughter. I told you about her. Remember?"

"Um, yes, that's right. Nice to meet you, Júlia." Sofia shook her hand.

"My dad asked me to bring you to your room tonight," Júlia said. She turned and skipped back up the stairs. Júlia seemed to have no cares in the world. Sofia wished she could skip up the stairs, but she had lots to worry about. Plus she was carrying her bag. It was light, but not that light.

At the top of the stairs, a small dirt path wound its way through the thick trees. The lush green leaves, twisted vines, and dense underbrush reminded her of the Jonathan Dickinson State Park near her grandparent's house. Florida seemed filled with high rises, homes, golf courses, and strip malls. But there were many wild areas too. Maybe not as wild as this though. This was the Amazon rainforest. You couldn't get much wilder than that.

Squawk! Yelp! Yelp! Yelp!

Júlia and Sofia whirled around. Their wide eyes searched the treetops. Sofia had heard this sound before.

"Look, it's a toucan." Júlia pointed to a brightly colored bird up in the tree.

Squawk! Yelp! Yelp! Yelp! SQUAWK!

"Tucano! Silêncio!" Júlia scolded. She shook her head and smirked.

The Troubled Toucan

"That looks like the same toucan that was hopping along while we were on the boat," Sofia said. "It's like he's following me." A small shiver ran down her spine.

He suddenly leaned in toward the girls. His beady eyes shifted as he looked at them. Squawk! Yelp! Yelp! Yelp! SQUAWWWK! The toucan jerked his bill and tail wildly with each call.

"*Uf! Tucano!* Geez! He is a troubled one," Júlia said. She grabbed Sofia's arm and headed farther up the path.

The toucan darted in and out of the trees next to them. He kept moving closer and closer. Squawk! Yelp! Yelp! Yelp! SQUAWK! His eerie call echoed in the rainforest.

"Is he chasing us?" Sofia walked even faster. She wished she could ditch her bag so she could run. "Do they do this a lot? Will he bite us?"

Júlia kept pace behind her. "*Não.* No, he will

not bite you. *Não se preocupe.* Don't worry." Her light-hearted voice was reassuring.

Sofia slowed down. She stole a quick glance behind her to see if the toucan still followed them.

Squawk! Yelp! Yelp! Yelp! SQUAWK! Yelp! Yelp! Yelp! SQUAWWWK! What was this bird's problem?

"Sofie-Bear, where is your inner bear?" Mr. Diaz called out up the path. "It's just a bird!"

"A really crazy one," Sofia yelled back. She put her head down and walked quickly up the path. The toucan hopped from tree to tree behind her, urging her up the trail. The next thing she knew, she felt a quick tug on her arm.

"Yikes! It's got me!" Sofia screamed.

"Is just me," Júlia giggled holding on to Sofia's arm. "Here are the rooms. I had to stop you, or you would be sleeping in the rainforest tonight." Her grin widened.

Sofia was still panting. She picked up her head and took a quick look around. Dusk had settled in. The towering trees created a canopy over the rustic brown building. A cozy glow came from a window under the thatched roof.

"We are in this room." Júlia pointed to the door on the left. "You and your dad are in this room." Júlia opened the door on the right.

"*Obrigada*. Thanks, Júlia."

Sofia darted through the open door. Júlia

seemed super friendly, but Sofia couldn't wait to get inside and away from that raving mad toucan.

She plopped her bags on the floor and turned around. The wooden walls glowed from the light of a small lamp. Two simple beds with neat white sheets stood along the walls. Across the room, a full wall of screens revealed the dense green trees of the rainforest. Then she saw the hammock.

"Dad! A hammock! There's a hammock in the room!" Sofia ran and jumped in the hammock. "Ah, now this is relaxing. No creepy guy. No crazy bird. Can I just stay here the whole time?"

"I'm afraid it would be hard to see the Amazon rainforest from your hammock," Mr. Diaz laughed. "You don't want to miss those beautiful blue morpho butterflies."

Maybe she couldn't see the Amazon rainforest swinging in the hammock, but she could certainly hear it. As the darkness set in, the noise grew louder.

Ribbet. Bzzzz. Bzzzz. Ribbet. Cricket. Bzzzz.

It sounded like the animals of the rainforest were all trying to talk to one another, but at the same exact time. Or like a chorus was warming up for a huge Amazon concert. She'd heard some of these sounds before in Florida. But some . . .

Screech. Grunt. Hsssss. Squawwwk!

Some were just alarming.

Chapter 4

Into the Igarapé

Even with all the scary sounds of the rainforest at night, Sofia slept like a rock. She woke up starving. Thank goodness the dining room was a quick walk down the path.

"*Bom Dia,* Sofia! Good morning," Júlia called from across the room. She was already eating breakfast at one of the tables near the edge of the room. The dining room's open sides and knotty log beams made it feel like they were eating outside.

Bushy jade-green leaves framed Júlia. Long brown grass from the thatched roof hung above her.

"Bom Dia!" Sofia called back. "Dad, I'm going to sit with Júlia, okay?"

"That's fine. I'm going to grab some fruit and go help Paulo get the canoes ready. I'll meet you down at the dock," Mr. Diaz replied as he left.

Sofia picked up some granola, açai berry yogurt, orange juice, and *pão francês,* a French roll toasted with butter. She could have been eating at home with a breakfast like this.

When Sofia sat down, Júlia's triangular face lit up with a smile. Her eyes twinkled playfully. She reached up and rearranged the clip in her hair, trying to get all of her wavy strands in the clip. A few small strands fell back down into her face. She shrugged and smiled.

"Me gusta tu camisa," Sofia said, using her Spanish. She figured Júlia might understand that she

meant she liked her shirt. The two languages had some similarities.

"Obrigada," Júlia smiled wider and looked down at her bright peach-colored tank top. "And, you say *'eu gosto de sua camisa'* in *Português.* Is close though. Spanish and Portuguese may be similar in some ways, but they have many differences too." She chuckled.

Sofia blushed. "Your English is better than my Portuguese.

Where did you learn it?" Sofia asked.

"I study English at school," Júlia replied. "And my dad speaks it to me. He speaks English to the people he works with from other countries, like your dad. Where did you learn your Spanish?"

"My grandparents came from Cuba, so my parents learned Spanish from them. They wanted to make sure we learned it too, so they speak Spanish to us at home most of the time."

"*Legal.* Cool," Júlia replied. She flashed a quick grin as she finished her last bite. "Ready to go?" She bounced up from her chair.

"Yup, *vamos!*"

Júlia chuckled again. "That one is similar to Spanish. Yes, let's go."

Sofia had to half-jog to keep up with Júlia's happy-go-lucky skip down the path. When they turned the corner, she could see her dad standing on the dock. Next to him, a small man was fixing something on the side of the old building. He wore a tan shirt loaded with pockets and blue cargo shorts. He had a coil of white rope hanging down from his right pocket.

"*Estamos aqui!* We are here!" Júlia announced to the dads. She stopped short at the first canoe.

"Ouch!" Sofia exclaimed, as she slammed right into Júlia's back.

Plop! Her sunglasses tumbled right off her head into the water. "Oh no!"

"*Não se preocupe,*" the man said. He jumped into the water up to his thighs. The bottom of his shorts got wet, but he didn't seem to mind. He reached down into the water and picked up the sinking glasses. As he handed them to Sofia, she noticed his round face, bright smile, and warm brown eyes.

"*Obrigada!* Thank you! Thank you so much," Sofia smiled. "*Meu nome é Sofia. Prazer em conhecé-lo,*" Sofia said practicing her Portuguese.

"De nada. Meu nome é Marcos," the man replied.

"This isn't your dad?" Sofia looked at Júlia, puzzled. She had heard her dad talk on the phone with Júlia's dad many times. She knew his name was Paulo. This man said he was Marcos, not Paulo.

"No, I'm Júlia's dad." Senhor Santos stepped out from behind the old building where he was loading the canoes. "Marcos works here at the lodge." He nodded his head at Marcos and then stuck out his hand to Sofia. "Nice to finally meet you. Your dad has told me so much about you."

Sofia blushed and shook his hand. *"Prazer em conhecé-lo.* Nice to meet you too."

"Vamos! Let's go. Hop in." Júlia pulled Sofia toward the canoe.

Into the Igarapé

Sofia hesitated. "Um, shouldn't we each be riding with our dads?" Sofia thought back to the caiman, the piranhas, and the anacondas.

"*Não.* No, we will paddle right next to them. Is more fun on our own. *Não se preocupe.* Don't worry!" She dragged Sofia into the canoe. Sofia wondered if Júlia ever worried about anything.

Mr. Diaz and Senhor Santos stepped into the second canoe. They paddled out of the little dock area and around the corner to the right.

Sofia loved all the colors of the Amazon. She took a mental picture in her mind. She wanted to remember the swirling black water of the Rio Negro, the vibrant green of the rainforest trees, and the deep blue of the bright daytime sky.

"Let's head down this *igarapé*," Senhor Santos said. "An *igarapé* is a narrow creek. During the rainy season, the islands and forests of the Anavilhanas Archipelago flood. They create what we call *igapós,* or flooded forests. If you come during the dry season, there are probably 400 islands. It's the world's largest fresh water archipelago."

"What's an archipelago?" Sofia asked Júlia.

"A group of islands," she answered. "Someday I want to become an Amazon ranger for these islands."

"What does a ranger do?"

"The rangers guard the rainforest *and* all of the animals in it. There are many animals here to take care of. There are birds, monkeys, butterflies, jaguars, and even poison dart frogs. They all need someone to look after them."

They paddled deeper through the flooded trees and vines. As the creek got smaller and smaller, the rainforest seemed to get thicker and thicker.

Senhor Santos stopped and pointed toward the top of a tree. "A sloth."

Sofia stared intently at the sloth hanging upside

down from the tree. She had heard sloths didn't move very fast. He didn't move at all. The black around his eyes made him look like a bandit. His mouth turned up in a smile. His fur looked . . . green? Sofia scrunched her eyes shut and opened them again. "Is his fur really green or is that my eyes?"

"It's really a light brown," Senhor Santos replied. "But they look green. They are so slow that algae from the trees builds up on their coats."

"What about the poison dart frogs?" Sofia asked. The sloths were clearly too slow to cause her any harm, but the poison dart frogs . . . well, she didn't know about the poison dart frogs. And she really needed to know in case she ran into one.

"Keep your eyes open. If we are lucky, we may see one along the side," Júlia said.

Lucky? Sofia thought running into one would not be so lucky. "I mean, do we need to be worried they will dart out at us with their poison?" Sofia's voice quivered.

"Não, não," Júlia giggled. "I mean, yes, they do have poison. But no, *não se preocupe,* don't worry. A long time ago, the native Indian people put poison from the frogs on the tip of their blow-dart weapons. Is why they call them poison dart frogs. But they can only poison you if you touch them with a cut on your skin."

Sofia felt a little bit better. For a moment.

Squawk! Yelp! Yelp! Yelp! SQUAWK!

The two girls jumped in their seats. The canoe rocked.

The toucan was back. And he didn't seem any happier than the day before.

Squawk! Yelp! Yelp! Yelp! SQUAWWWK!

Sofia spun the canoe away from the toucan. But he just darted from tree to tree following them. Júlia started paddling too. Her relaxed manner seemed to disappear with the troubled toucan hot on their trail.

Squawk! Yelp! Yelp! Yelp! SQUAWK! Yelp! Yelp! Yelp! SQUAWWWK!

"Over there! Down that creek to the right!" Sofia pointed. The girls swiftly paddled down a narrow creek. Sweat was dripping down Sofia's back now. The canopy above them grew thicker, blocking out the sun. Twisted tree trunks encircled them.

Squawk! Yelp! Yelp! Yelp! SQUAWK! Yelp! Yelp! Yelp! SQUAWWWK! The toucan chased them farther and farther down the eerie creek.

"Keep paddling, Júlia!"

"Uf! Geeez, I *am* paddling."

Squawk! Yelp! Yelp Yelp! SQUAWK! The toucan hopped in front of the girls. He looked at them. Then he quietly half-yelped as if to say sorry.

The girls looked at each other, confused.

"Why did he stop?"

"Não sei. I don't know." Júlia shook her head.

A movement by the side of the creek caught Sofia's eye. She sucked in her breath. Her eyes opened wide.

"What?" Júlia asked in a low voice.

"Something moved over there. Under the water. Near the edge of the creek," Sofia squeaked. "Do you think it's a caiman . . . or an anaconda?"

"I hope not." As quiet as a mouse, Júlia put her paddle in the water. Sofia was sure they needed to splash the water and sound more like a bear, but she followed Júlia's lead and kept quiet. A grey and pink speckled head popped up out of the water.

"Botos. Pink dolphins." Júlia sighed with relief.

"Pink dolphins?" Sofia exclaimed loudly. She had always wanted to see pink dolphins. She had read about them in social studies at school. She knew they were rare and endangered.

"Psiu! Shhhh!" Júlia turned around and put

her finger to her mouth.

"Will we scare them away?" Sofia whispered.
Maybe her big mouth just blew her only chance to
see pink dolphins.

"I think they are tied up."

They paddled a little closer. Yup. Sure enough,
three dirty white ropes held three pink dolphins
by their flukes, the fins on the end of their bodies.
Their long, straight beaks were bumping into each
other. They looked different than the dolphins in

Miami. The dorsal fins on their backs were smaller. And they glowed an orange color in the water. One stuck his head up and looked at Sofia. His eyes were sad.

"Why would they be tied up?" Sofia murmured.

"Poachers." Júlia's eyes clouded under her furrowed eyebrows. Her lips pressed together in a thin, straight line. "This never used to happen. Amazon folklore said that the *boto* was, how do you say, *encantado.*"

"Enchanted?"

"*Sim.* Yes. *Botos* would lead people to a magical underwater city. But now the poachers don't care about folklore. Now, they care about money. They capture *botos* to use as bait to catch other fish that they can sell. They are mean and greedy. The rangers try to stop them. But there are not enough to guard everywhere in the Amazon." Her eyes watered up.

Into the Igarapé

Clearly, Júlia did have things she worried about, Sofia thought. And the animals of the Amazon were one of those things.

The water rippled. The trees rustled. The toucan yelped.

"We need to get out of here," Júlia said. *"Vamos!"*

Sofia sensed danger. She looked around. The dark green trees of the rainforest seemed to lean in even more, as if to trap her. And the snaking black vines looked like long scrawny fingers reaching out to grab her.

She needed her dad. But they were all alone.

Chapter 5

Out of the Igarapé

"Oh no! Where did our dads go?" Sofia jabbed frantically at the water with her paddle. She couldn't turn the canoe around fast enough.

"Psiu!" Júlia yelled in her loudest whisper voice. "If the poachers are nearby, we don't want them to hear us!"

Good point, Sofia thought. She put her paddle in and out of the water as softly and quietly as she could. But still as fast as she could. The canoe glided silently down the creek.

"Hey, there's the toucan again," Sofia whispered.

Júlia looked to the side of the creek. The toucan hopped along with them from tree to tree. He looked sad, but he didn't squawk or yelp at them. It was as if he knew they needed to be quiet.

The girls paddled on. Softly. Quietly. Quickly. They turned one corner. Then another. No dads. They kept paddling, trying not to panic.

Sofia's heart had moved from her chest to her throat. She really, really wanted her dad to be here with her. Right now. Was this what it would feel like when he wasn't around at home? She gulped down a sob.

Then they turned the corner and saw two frowning dads across the way. Sofia's heart flooded with relief.

"Where have you two been? You paddled off so quickly, we lost you. We've been looking for fifteen minutes!" Mr. Diaz yelled.

Only fifteen minutes? It had seemed like fifteen hours.

"The toucan. He was chasing us again. He . . . He . . ." Sofia burst into tears.

Mr. Diaz's face softened. "Aw, Sofie-Bear. It's okay." He pulled the two canoes together and put his arm around her shoulders.

Mr. Santos gave Júlia a questioning look. *"Juju?"*

Júlia looked down at her hands. *"O tucano nos*

42

assustou, Pai. Desculpe," Júlia murmured. The toucan had scared her too. "Sorry."

"Dad, I was so scared when I realized you weren't there," Sofia blubbered.

"Me too, Sofia. But I knew we would find you. You know, I'll *always* be there for you," Mr. Diaz reassured.

"Will you? Really?" Sofia said under her breath.

"I heard that, Sofia. And yes, I will be. Things may be a little different when we get back home, but I will always be there for you," Mr. Diaz said. He wiped a tear from his eye. "I think that's enough for today, don't you, Paulo?"

Senhor Santos nodded. *"Sim.* Yes. Let's head back."

They paddled down the creek to the river.

"Dad, there were pink dolphins back there. Tied up. Júlia said they were from poachers."

"Botos? Caçadores furtivos? Is that what Júlia

said?" Senhor Santos seemed annoyed. "Júlia, I know you want to be a ranger, but you must stop making up these stories when we visit the Anavilhanas."

Senhor Santos turned to Mr. Diaz. "I'm sorry. Júlia is always coming up with stories where she can be the ranger and save the animals. She probably dragged Sofia down that creek to create a ranger story."

"No, Dad, really, we saw them," Sofia insisted.

"*Nós os vimos, Pai.* We did see them, Dad." Júlia shook her head sadly. Senhor Santos looked back at Mr. Diaz and rolled his eyes. Mr. Diaz chuckled.

Sofia started to protest again, but then her dad gave her the "be quiet" look. The conversation was clearly over. The girls paddled back to the dock in silence.

As they got out of their canoes, Júlia pulled Sofia aside.

"Is not right," Júlia whispered. Her voice stayed low, but firm and forceful.

"What's not right?"

"Leaving the *botos* there. A ranger would not leave the *botos* there to die," Júlia said. "We need to go back and save them. We need to get there before the poachers do. We may be their last chance at freedom."

"How are we going to get there? We were just totally lost in the creeks." Sofia looked doubtful. "And we can't take a canoe out by ourselves. And it's not like they left us a map or anything."

"We don't need a canoe. Or a map. We have *o tucano.*" Júlia pointed to the trees next to her. The toucan sat on a low branch. His brightly colored beak stood out against the tangle of dark green rainforest leaves. He tilted his head to the side. Beady eyes stared back at Sofia.

Squawk! Sofia jumped. Her heart skipped a beat.

The toucan squawked again. But it was more of a whine. Not the urgent, troubled yelping from earlier.

"Don't you see?" Júlia pressed on.

"See what?"

"*O tucano.* He is not crazy. He is worried about the *botos!* He has been saying help, help, help!"

"I'm not so sure about that." Sofia folded her arms across her chest and pressed her lips tightly together. "You really think so?"

"*Confie em mim.* Trust me," Júlia said. "*O tucano* will lead us. We must do this. We must save the *botos.* If we don't do this, who will?"

"The rangers? Couldn't we just call the rangers?"

Júlia shook her head. "The Amazon is huge, and there are not enough rangers. It could take them days to get here. We are their only hope."

Chapter 6

Dolphin Rescue

The toucan hopped from tree to tree ahead of them. They followed him, winding their way down a small worn path.

"Are you sure this is safe?" Sofia was certain it wasn't. They were, after all, in the Amazon.

Júlia nodded her head. *"Não se preocupe.* Don't worry. I have walked around the lodge area a lot. Just keep your eyes open."

"Keep my eyes open for what?" Sofia asked.

She wasn't sure she wanted to know the answer. But she needed to know. How else could she plan an escape?

"Mostly snakes. Maybe some spiders," Júlia replied coolly.

Sofia shuddered. The best plan for this, she thought, would be to run. Yup. Run. She realized that Júlia lived here so she was probably used to these sorts of things. Maybe that was why she was so calm all the time.

They continued on through the maze of twisted vines and overgrown bushes. Sofia kept her eyes open wide. Very wide. So far, so good.

Or not.

"Yikes! Is that a tarantula?" Sofia pointed to a tree off the side of the trail. Eight thick legs carried a big, hairy spider slowly up the tree trunk. A shiver ran all the way up Sofia's neck to the backs of her ears. And it kept going all the way down through her knees to her feet. "Run!"

Júlia grabbed Sofia's arm. "*Não!* Don't run. Tarantulas look scarier than they are. They can bite, but the bites don't kill people. Just stay away. Plus, we don't want the poachers to hear us if they are around."

Sofia stopped. She didn't like the tarantula, but she didn't want to run into the poachers either.

"*O igarapé!* The creek! I think the *botos* are here." Júlia pointed ahead.

They peered around the last few trees next to the creek. No poachers. And the pink dolphins still floated in the shallow water. Júlia got out her jackknife and knelt down. A dolphin looked up at her and bobbed his head up and down.

"What are you doing?"

"I will cut the ropes," Júlia replied.

"If you cut the ropes, the poachers will know someone was here. And maybe they'll come looking for us."

"Then what is *your* plan?"

"Let's just untie the ropes. The poachers will think they got loose," Sofia replied.

"How do we do that?"

"Piece of cake." Sofia rubbed her hands together.

"Piece of cake?" Júlia looked puzzled. "We eat cake now?"

"Sorry, it's a saying in English. It means it's easy. Simple. One of us can pull the dolphin in while the other one unties the rope from its tail."

"The *botos'* jaws are strong," Júlia warned.

"They could turn around and bite us." She raised her eyebrows.

"Okay, maybe not quite a piece of cake. But I know we can do it," Sofia said with her best Sofie-Bear voice.

The girls worked quickly. Júlia pulled each dolphin in with the rope tied to its fluke. Rubbing their backs, she tried to calm them down. *"Não se preocupe.* Don't worry."

Sofia untied the knots while the dolphins squirmed and squirmed. The toucan hopped from tree to tree around them. He moved his giant beak from one side to the other. His eyes scanned the trees. He wasn't so scary now. In fact, it seemed to Sofia that he was guarding them.

"Just one more knot, and we've got it." Sofia let out a big sigh. She realized she'd been holding her breath.

The last dolphin wiggled away, gliding through

Mystery of the Troubled Toucan

the grooved trunks of the flooded trees. He curled
around and flapped his tail as if to say, "thank you!"
Then he darted away to freedom.

"*Oba!* Yay! We did it!" Júlia cheered in a
whisper. She reached out and hugged Sofia. The
toucan hopped happily around them. No squawks
or yelps now.

But another noise interrupted the celebration.
Putt. Putt. Putt. Sputter. Putt. Putt. Putt.

The girls looked at each other and scrambled
into the shelter of the dense trees. They followed
a smaller path alongside the creek. They could still
hear the boat engine, but they couldn't see it. Sofia
thought that was just fine. She hoped the boat
could not see them either. As they rounded the next
corner, the trees opened up to the Rio Negro.

The girls knelt down and peeked through the
leaves. An old blue boat slithered slowly down the
river. The lingering light of the early evening made

it hard for them to see too much.

"Do you think those are the poachers?" Sofia asked.

"*Não sei*. I don't know. If they are, we should get out of here," Júlia said. She nervously brushed a strand of hair away from her face. "Plus, we don't want to be out here after dark."

"Yup. Right. Let's go then," Sofia wanted to get out of the rainforest before it was too dark to see the snakes. Or the spiders. Or any other animals they could stumble upon in the darkness of the Amazon at night.

The girls followed the small path as it wound along next to the creek, then into the rainforest, and then down by the creek again.

"I think we are going in circles," Júlia confessed.

Sofia's heart skipped a beat when she realized they were lost in the Amazon. By themselves.

Again. "Where's the toucan now?" she growled.

"*Pare!* Stop! I hear something." Júlia pressed her arm back on Sofia's shoulder.

"What? I don't hear anything. I especially don't hear a 'squawk' now that we need it."

Branches snapped. Leaves crunched.

"Someone is coming!" Júlia insisted.

They tiptoed around the corner and a dark shadow stood over them.

The shadow stepped back, surprised at the sight of the two girls. Then it moved in closer.

The girls shrank back. Sofia didn't want to shrink back too far—into a tree, or a spider, or a snake. She didn't know whether to keep her eyes on the shadow or the darkness behind her.

The shadow spoke rapidly in Portuguese to Júlia. She replied. He spoke again.

"Is Marcos!" Júlia hugged Sofia. "He asked what we are doing out here so close to dark. I said we were walking and got lost. I asked him if he could guide us to the lodge."

"Oh, thank you, thank you, thank you!" Sofia's heartbeat slowed back to normal.

Júlia leaned in a little closer to Sofia and whispered in her ear, "I did not tell him what we were *really* doing. I did not want us to get in trouble with our dads."

As they walked, Marcos talked with Júlia and she translated for Sofia.

"I asked him why he was out here. He said he came to check on some things for the lodge."

Sofia looked at Marcos. He smiled and nodded his head. His warm eyes sparkled in the light of his flashlight. Sofia felt safe with his friendly tone and manner. He had tools in the pockets of his shorts that made a clanging noise when he walked. And something swung back and forth from his belt loop. Sofia wondered if it was a big knife. She guessed he needed all these tools to do his repair work.

Marcos asked Júlia a question. She answered, and he chuckled.

Júlia turned to Sofia. "He asked me what I like to do in Manaus. I told him I like to go on adventures and play with animals, but not snakes. I hate snakes."

Sofia smiled and nodded her head in agreement. Marcos asked Júlia another question.

"He wants to know what you like to do in the United States, Sofia," Júlia said.

"I like to swim and play in the ocean. I also really like gymnastics. I drive my dad crazy because I do cartwheels everywhere," Sofia smiled. She put her arms up to do a cartwheel. Then she looked at the dark path ahead of her and put them down again. "Well, maybe not everywhere." She shrugged her shoulders and added, "I like adventures and animals too. I don't have a rainforest full of animals to hang out with like you do, though."

Júlia told Marcos what Sofia said. His smile grew wider. He talked some more. Then Júlia spoke, waving her arms about. Marcos chuckled again.

"He likes to hike in the rainforest and bring people on adventures. He said maybe one day he could bring our families on an adventure with him. I told him he might not want to bring my family. I have two brothers and three sisters. My little brother, Bruno, is a crazy boy who chases people all over. And my sister Amanda likes to boss everyone around."

"Wow, that's a big family," Sofia said. "I have an older brother and a younger brother. And they are both pretty annoying." She scowled.

"I guess brothers and sisters can be a pain everywhere in the world," Júlia said with a grin.

They both giggled.

"Does he have a family?" Sofia asked.

Júlia asked Marcos. He smiled and nodded. He took a picture from his pocket to show them as he spoke.

Júlia translated. "This is his little girl, Mariana. He calls her Marianita. She is three. His wife is going to have another baby soon too. He loves them very much. He works hard to take care of them." She handed Sofia the picture.

Sofia squinted through the fading light. A sweet little face framed by loose brown curls stared out at her from the worn picture. A nice family, Sofia thought. What would happen to her own family when her dad moved out? She wished she knew the answers. She wished she knew how to fix things.

They rounded the last corner to the lodge. Sofia looked back at the rainforest as the darkness closed in. It seemed like darkness was closing in everywhere in her life right now.

"Muito, muito obrigada," Sofia said politely. "Thank you very, very much." She gave Marcos a quick hug. Maybe she should have given him a bigger one. But she felt sad and tired. He did, however, save them from a scary night in the Amazon. But she didn't really know him *that* well.

Chapter 7

Plan A

"I'm not going to hide in a rainforest full of snakes and spiders at night to wait for some dangerous poachers." Sofia said, scrunching her eyebrows.

The girls were walking back from lunch the next day. Sofia's mouth was still tingling from the *tacacá* they just ate. *Tacacá* was a soup made with *tucupi*, a root that was poisonous. Sofia had thought that seemed a bit dangerous. But her dad slurped up a mouthful and was still alive. So she took a bite too. Then her mouth started to go numb, and she panicked. As usual, Júlia had chimed in and told her not worry. But she'd been sure she was being poisoned. Then her dad had explained that they cooked the poison out. And that the *jambú* leaves they used numb your mouth. It wasn't poison. He had winked at her and told her it was all part of the experience.

After all that, she was really looking forward to crashing in her hammock before the evening boat tour. Going back into the Amazon for the night was NOT part of her plan.

"We must do something," Júlia pleaded. "A ranger would not just free the *botos*. A ranger would catch the poachers so they don't do it again!"

"Reminder. We aren't rangers. Why don't we just call the rangers and report this," Sofia argued.

"I called them this morning, but it will take hours, maybe days, for them to get here. We need to catch the poachers before they catch more *botos.*"

"Well, we need a different plan."

"Like what?"

"I'm thinking," Sofia said. She rubbed her chin with her thumb and index finger. "I have an idea."

Sofia grabbed Júlia's hand and pulled her into her room. She found her dad's bag and dug through it.

"What are you doing?" Júlia asked. *"Tem macaquinhos em sua cabeça."*

"What? Did you say something about my head?" Sofia asked. She shoved something into her pocket.

"I said you have little monkeys in your head."

"Monkeys? I don't see any monkeys here."

"Não. In your head!" Júlia's eyes sparkled. "Is a Brazilian saying. It means something like you have strange ideas in your head."

"Not so strange if they can save the dolphins," Sofia giggled. *"Vamos!* Off to the *botos!* Where's our little troubled toucan?"

"Tucano, onde você está?" Júlia whistled. "Where are youuuu?" The toucan hopped out from behind a bush.

Squawk!

"Can you show us the way again?" Júlia asked.

"And this time, you need to stick around and lead us back," Sofia added.

Squawk! Squawk! The toucan started hopping down the trail.

Sofia and Júlia marched around the bushes, leaves, vines, and trees on the path they walked the day before. This time, though, rays of sunshine broke through the rainforest's canopy to light the way. Sofia felt much better about this plan. The girls tiptoed the last few steps to the clearing where the dolphins had been tied up.

"So, what did you get from your dad's bag?" Júlia asked.

"This," Sofia said, holding up his cell phone. "We can tie it to a tree and put the video on. It should record anyone who comes here."

"*Bem!* Good job!" Júlia smiled brightly. "We can show the video to the rangers when they get here." Then her smile faded. "But will your dad get mad?"

Sofia shook her head. "Nah. Not too much. He's used to us taking his phone to play games. Plus, he's on vacation. I doubt he'll even notice."

Sofia grabbed a piece of rope that had been used to tie up the dolphins. Júlia looked for the perfect tree.

"This tree will work," Júlia said. "No spiders or snakes. And you can see the place where the *botos* had been from here."

Sofia wrapped the rope around the tree and tied it. Then Júlia stuck the bottom of the phone under the rope to hold it in place.

"Now, we just need to turn the video on and check it tomorrow." Sofia reached over and pressed the record button.

The toucan half-yelped. He pointed his beak up the path. Then he started hopping from tree to tree toward the lodge. He seemed happy to lead the way back. And the girls were very happy to follow.

Chapter 8

Boats in the Night

"Boa noite, meu nome é Tinho," the tour guide said.
"Good evening, my name is Tinho," he translated
into English. "I am happy to show you the *igapós*
at night." Senhor Santos had arranged for them to
take a night boat tour of the flooded forests. Sofia
and Mr. Diaz climbed into the seats in front of Júlia
and her dad.

Tinho motored the boat away from dock and
down the Rio Negro. As the sun set, the sky turned

shades of orange and purple. Blue and yellow macaws flew overhead. They looked like jewels in the dusky sky. The still water reflected the dark trees on each side of the river.

Sofia thought this time of night was always beautiful in Florida too. But the bugs took the fun out of it. No-see-ums, mosquitoes—

"Um, where are the mosquitoes? We're in the rainforest. There should be mosquitoes, right?"

"You would think so. But no." Senhor Santos shook his head once. "There aren't many mosquitoes here. When the forest floods, the brush and vegetation under the water rots. This creates a lot of acid in the water. The acid in the water makes it hard for mosquitoes to breed."

Sofia thought that was one of the best things she'd heard in a long time. No mosquitoes. Maybe things were looking up.

They turned down a small creek. The animals

of the Amazon were tuning up their vocal chords for the evening's eerie chorus. The trees of the flooded forest now towered darkly over them on each side. Sofia shuddered.

"Look!" Júlia pointed to something hanging from a tree.

"*Sim*, an emerald tree boa." Tinho's flashlight lit up the green snake wrapped three times around the branch. Chills ran up and down Sofia's spine. Her eyes followed the light as it drifted down the tree to the water. A pair of red eyes glowed in the murky water. She squirmed backwards in her seat and squeezed in tighter next to her dad.

"*O jacaré*. A caiman," Tinho whispered eagerly. He steered the boat closer and then turned the motor off. The boat drifted toward the caiman. He lurked under the shadowy tree draped with the boa. Sofia couldn't slide any farther back in her seat, so she pulled her knees to her chest.

Tinho leaned over in the water and reached in.

Sofia drew in a quick breath. "What's he doing?"

"Catching a caiman," Júlia said. Tinho pulled a baby caiman out of the water and into the boat.

Sofia almost jumped on top of her dad's lap. She definitely would have if Júlia hadn't been sitting right behind her. But she didn't. After all, she was a bear, not a mouse. And she wanted to be sure Júlia knew that.

Tinho held out the baby caiman for them to touch. Júlia reached over and stroked its spiny back.

"Come on, Sofia. *Não se preocupe*. Try it. How often do you get to touch a caiman?"

Only once in her life probably, Sofia thought. She looked at the baby caiman. His dark eyes glared at her, daring her to touch him. She took a deep gulp and reached over Júlia to place her index finger on the caiman's back. She was definitely a bear now she thought proudly.

Tinho gently placed the baby caiman into the water and turned the boat around. They glided back through the flooded trees.

Putt. Putt. Sputter. Putt. Putt.

Sofia tilted her head toward the sound. As they glided out of the *igarapé* she could see a blue boat floating slowly across their path. Dirty white ropes hung over the side.

Sofia spun around. She and Júlia exchanged looks. Júlia raised her eyebrows and mouthed, "The same boat?" Sofia nodded. She turned back around to take another look.

"Can I borrow your camera for a moment,

Dad? I just want to get a better look at the birds over there."

"Sure thing, Sofie-Bear," Mr. Diaz replied.

As she slowly turned the zoom lens, she understood why it seemed so familiar. Black eyes peered out from under a dirty blue hat. The man turned to speak to the other three people on the boat. Then the boat sped up and took a sharp turn down the creek next to the lodge.

"Figures! I don't know why I didn't think of it sooner!" Sofia exclaimed. She shoved the camera back into her dad's hands. Turning around, she pulled Júlia closer to her so that their heads were touching.

"It's creepy Hugo, the boat driver who

brought us to the lodge," Sofia whispered. "I think he made his boat break down so he could rob us. But we fixed it and spoiled his plans. He's the poacher. He and his thief friends."

"Are you sure?" Júlia wrinkled her brows.

"Has to be. Didn't you see the way he sped off down the creek, right toward where the pink dolphins were? Plus, he had dirty white ropes hanging over the side. Like the ones we found tied to the dolphins. And his thief friends were with him."

Júlia bit her lower lip. She nodded slowly.

Sofia had wished she would never run into creepy Hugo again. But it looked like her wish wasn't going to come true. She hugged her knees tightly and curled in a little closer to her dad as the boat glided back through the black waters of the Rio Negro.

Chapter 9

Plan B

Sofia followed Júlia down the path. The toucan hopped along beside her. She felt good having two Amazon friends, even if one was a bird.

"Over here," Júlia said in her loudest whisper voice. She let out a large sigh and her shoulders slumped. "The battery is dead," she said.

But Sofia had expected that. She held up her dad's extra battery case. Júlia beamed. *"Bravo!"*

Sofia plugged the phone into the battery-powered case and pushed the power button.

Júlia shifted from one foot to the other, waiting. "Is it on yet?"

"Sometimes it takes a bit to power up. There we go . . ." Sofia hit the play button on the last video. She held her breath.

They could hear the sounds of the Amazon chorus loud and clear.

"I see nothing!" Júlia said. She grabbed at the phone to tilt it toward her.

"That's because there is nothing to see," Sofia sighed. "It's black. Pitch black. I can't believe it. I really thought this plan would work."

"The canopy of the rainforest is too dark. What are we going to do now?" Júlia wondered aloud.

"I don't know," Sofia said. "Go have lunch?" Her stomach growled.

"We cannot let them get away," Júlia persisted. "We need another plan."

Sofia closed her eyes and rubbed the bridge of her nose. Another plan. Another plan. Another plan.

"Maybe we could dig a deep hole and cover it with leaves. When they walk over it, they'll fall in and be trapped. Or we could set up a trip wire with a net on the ground that could scoop them up."

Júlia snorted. "Even if we could do any of those, where would we get things like that in the Amazon? We should wait out here tonight to see if we can catch them."

"No way. No." Sofia shook her head. "NO. We are NOT going into the Amazon in the middle of the night. Not going to happen. But we could . . ." Sofia looked at the phone in her hand. She pressed a few more buttons. Then she placed it gently on the ground near the white ropes.

"What are you doing now?" Júlia raised an eyebrow. "More monkeys in your head?"

"You'll see," Sofia said with a singsong voice.

Plan B

She grabbed Júlia's hand and pulled her down the path toward the lodge. "Let's go have lunch."

As they entered the dining room, Sofia saw her dad running his hands through his hair. Uh-oh. He was stressed out.

"Where have you been?" Mr. Diaz asked as they entered the dining room. "I've been looking all over for you!" He threw his hands up in the air.

"Sorry, Dad," Sofia mumbled. "We just took

a quick walk." She looked down at her feet.

"You can't be running off here in the Amazon. It's too dangerous," Mr. Diaz scolded. "You need to tell me where you're going."

"You need to tell *me* where *you're* going," Sofia blurted out.

"Excuse me?" Mr. Diaz said, surprised.

"What I meant was, I . . . I'm as worried about you leaving as you are about me," Sofia said.

"I guess we're both worried," Mr. Diaz said. "But *you*, my Sofie-Bear, you do *not* need to worry. I am *not* leaving you. I'm just going to be living in a separate place. I'll still be your dad. I'll still help you with your homework. I'll still be at your gymnastics meets. And I'll still be worrying about *you!*" Mr. Diaz said. He gave Sofia a hug.

"Thanks, Dad," Sofia said. She hugged him back tightly. She felt safe and secure and didn't want to let go.

Chapter 10

The Unexpected Decision

The next morning Sofia woke up to the yelp of a toucan. Was it her toucan? She wasn't sure. But now that she was awake, she remembered what she needed to do.

As quiet as a mouse, she reached over to the pile of clothes next to her bed. She pulled on the clothes she wore the day before. Then she put her dad's laptop in her bag and tiptoed out the door.

She tapped on the screen next to Júlia's bed.

"Júlia, pssst! Wake up."

Júlia stirred but didn't open her eyes.

"Pssst! Júlia! Pssst! Get up!" She tapped on the screen again.

Júlia opened one eye. Then she bolted straight up and opened her mouth as if to scream.

"Shhhh! Júlia, it's just me. Let's go eat breakfast," Sofia whispered.

Júlia met Sofia outside. She was still rubbing her eyes.

"Why are we up so early?"

"The toucan woke me up. I think he wants us to see if our plan worked."

Júlia looked puzzled. She shrugged her shoulders and followed along. At the breakfast table, Sofia pulled her dad's laptop out of her bag.

"What are you doing with your dad's laptop?" Júlia looked worried.

"It's part of my plan. My dad uses this cool app

to track which one of us kids is using his phone," Sofia said. "It takes pictures of people who enter the wrong password. Then it emails the pictures to him. He thinks he's being super sneaky, but we all know about it." Sofia smiled. She opened up the laptop and started clicking around. "The best part? The camera's flash goes off if it's too dark. Hopefully, the lodge's satellite Internet reaches as far as the creek and the email will work."

"I guess we will find out," Júlia said.

Sofia opened up her dad's email. She drew in a quick breath.

"What? Do you see something?"

"It's an email from my mom." Sofia's eyes welled up with tears.

"What does it say?"

"It's apartment listings. My dad's moving out," Sofia choked.

"I'm sorry, Sofia." Júlia put her arm around

her new best friend. "I can tell that he loves you a lot. You will still be a family, maybe just a little different."

Sofia wasn't sure how you could be living separately and still be together like a family. "I guess I'll find out."

Sofia wiped her eyes and called on her inner bear to help her. "I can't think about that right now." She took a deep breath. "I'll figure out my plan for *that* problem after we solve *this* problem."

She scanned the rest of the emails at the top of the inbox. There it was.

"It worked! The email worked. And someone took the bait."

"Open it. See who it is!"

"I'm sure it's creepy Hugo." Sofia clicked on the email to open it. They both gasped.

"This can't be right!" Sofia stared at the photo.

"*Não.* No—" Júlia shook her head, stunned.

Staring back at them from the photo was the surprised face of sweet Marianita's dad, Marcos.

"What are we going to do?" Sofia groaned. She felt teary.

"What *should* we do?" Júlia moaned.

"I don't know. He's been so nice to us. It can't be him. It just can't be!" Sofia put her head in her hands. "Plus, he's a dad. If we report him, he'll go to jail. If he goes to jail, Marianita and the new baby won't have a dad." She thought of how upset she was about not being with her own dad. How could she take away Marianita's dad?

Júlia nodded slowly. Tears welled up in her eyes. "But what about the *botos?* They have families too. Marcos is catching mothers and fathers," Júlia

83

sniffled. *"Mau!* This is terrible."

Now Sofia nodded slowly. Tears rolled down her cheeks. This was definitely NOT what she expected. She would have no problem sending creepy Hugo off to jail. But Marcos? Sofia could not keep the tattered picture of sweet Marianita out of her mind. "He seemed like he was working so hard for his family. Do you think that's why he did this?"

"Não sei. I don't know. But I *do* know that if I ever want to be a ranger, we should report him," Júlia said firmly.

Sofia still wasn't sure what to do. "There must be another way. Another plan."

The girls sat in silence.

Then Júlia perked up. "This time, I think *I* have a plan."

Chapter 11

Plan C

The girls walked down to the dock. There wasn't a skip in their step this time, but there was hope. Marcos was fixing something on the old building again. He looked up, waved at the girls, and gave them a big smile. His smile faded as the ranger docked the boat and pulled in.

"Boa tarde, Júlia. Obrigado por seu telefonema," the ranger said to Júlia.

Júlia responded in Portuguese. The ranger said

something back. Then they both turned to look at Marcos.

Marcos slowly walked over to them. Then it was a jumble of Portuguese. First, the ranger spoke to Marcos. Then Marcos responded. Júlia jumped in next. Back to Marcos. He pulled something out of his pocket. The ranger said something else. Júlia chimed in again.

Sofia's head moved back and forth following

the conversation. She didn't really understand much
though. She hoped Júlia had a good plan. By the
pained look on Marcos' face, it didn't seem that way.

Then the owner of the lodge showed up. The
owner talked to the ranger. Then to Marcos. Júlia
talked to the owner. The owner nodded. Marcos'
face brightened. They all shook hands.

Júlia turned to Sofia with a broad grin. "It
worked. My plan worked!"

"What? What happened?" Sofia asked.

"Marcos admitted he tied up the *botos*," Júlia
started. "He said a man offered to pay him to catch
the *botos*. With the new baby coming, he really
needed the money to help feed his family."

Sofia frowned. "So, why are you happy? Isn't
Marcos going to jail for poaching?"

"No. He did not hurt the *botos*. He knew it
was not the right thing to do. So he decided to let
them go. He went to untie them, but he ran into us

instead. He tried again a few nights later. But when he got there, they were already gone." Júlia winked at Sofia. "He saw the phone and picked it up. He thought maybe the poachers found the *botos* and dropped their phone while they were untying them. He returned it to us just now." Júlia handed the cell phone back to Sofia.

"So what happens to Marcos?"

"The ranger gave him a warning," Júlia answered. "He swore he would never do anything to harm the Amazon animals again. You could see tears in his eyes. I think he meant it."

"And why is the lodge owner here?"

"Is the best part." Júlia's smile spread across her face. "After breakfast, I called the ranger again. I let him know we found the poacher. Then I told the lodge owner about Marcos. He was really mad. He wanted to fire Marcos right away. I said we should all wait to hear his side of the story."

Plan C

"And?"

"And once the owner heard the whole story, he knew Marcos was a good man. A man who made a bad decision but tried to make it right. He said he would give him another chance. So I told the owner that Marcos likes to take people on adventures. I said he should hire him as a tour guide. Then he would earn enough money to feed his family."

"And?"

"And, he agreed!" Júlia jumped up and down holding Sofia's hands. Sofia joined in. And then she stopped.

"But what about the *real* poachers? The ones who were going to pay him?"

"Marcos agreed to tell the poachers where he tied up the *botos*. *We* know the *botos* are not there. But *they* don't. The ranger is going to watch the area tonight. When they show up, he will catch them."

Chapter 12

Coming Together

"What's all the fuss about?" Mr. Diaz said as he marched into the dining room of the lodge. Senhor Santos followed behind. "We're about ready to board the seaplane to Manaus. Why did you girls want us to meet you here?"

The girls were whispering and laughing with each other.

The lodge owner and the ranger were standing at the front of the room. "This will only take a few minutes, sir," the lodge owner piped in. "And I promise it will be worth your time."

"Dad, Dad! Over here." Sofia patted the seat next to her. Her dad sat down. Senhor Santos followed and sat next to Júlia.

"Before you left, I wanted to take a few minutes to reward the good work of Sofia and Júlia," the ranger started. The lodge owner translated to English.

Mr. Diaz and Senhor Santos looked at each other, puzzled.

"Over the last few days, the girls found some *botos* tied up in the rainforest. Not only did they free the *botos*, but they also found the critical link to a ring of poachers we have been tracking in the Anavilhanas Archipelago."

Mr. Diaz looked at Senhor Santos. He raised his eyebrows. Senhor Santos shook his head and chuckled.

"I wanted to let everyone know that last night, we did catch them. It was a ring of poachers known as Hugo and the Hunters."

Sofia slapped her hands on her knees. "I knew it," she blurted out.

"They are in custody now thanks to the efforts of Sofia and Júlia," the ranger continued. "So I would like to present them both with these Amazon Junior Ranger badges. Good job, girls! And Júlia, I think you definitely have a future as an Amazon ranger!" The ranger winked at Júlia.

As the ranger pinned their badges on, Sofia heard a soft yelp, like a puppy whining for attention. She looked over at the window. The toucan sat on the railing. He nodded his head. She nudged Júlia and whispered, "No more loud squawks."

"No more trouble," Júlia replied. They giggled.

Senhor Santos stood up and gave Júlia a big hug. He smiled wide with pride. *"Bravo, JuJu!"*

"Well done, Sofie-Bear," Mr. Diaz said patting her on the back. "You always manage to figure things out. I'm so proud of you."

Coming Together

They left the lodge for the last time and boarded the seaplane. Sofia felt the metal badge on her shirt. It felt heavy and good. She and Júlia did manage to figure it out. She would miss her adventures with Júlia in the Amazon.

Júlia slid into the seat in front of Sofia. As the plane got closer to Manaus, she turned around and looked through the space between the seats.

"Here," she said. Júlia shoved a ribbon through the space in the seats. "To remember me and Brazil."

"What is it?" Sofia rubbed the cool, smooth ribbon between her fingers.

"Is a *fita*, a good luck bracelet. My dad brought it back from Salvador, another city in Brazil. I've been saving it to give to a special friend. Tie it around your wrist and make a wish. Don't cut it off or your wish will not come true. Let it fall off."

Sofia tied it around her wrist. She wished that she would still be best friends with Júlia even

though they were going to be apart. And then she
wished that she could figure out how to keep her
family together. She doubted that wish would come
true, even if the *fita* did fall off.

She let out a deep sigh, leaned her head against
the window of the plane and looked down. The
black waters of the Rio Negro and the brown
waters of the Rio Solimões seemed to flow right
next to each other, yet not mix.

"Wow, Dad, that's amazing," Sofia said turning
to her dad. She pointed out the window.

"Yes, that's the meeting of the waters, *Encontro
das Aguas*. Together those separate rivers make up
the Amazon. They are separate but together. That's
us," he said. "Each of us is like the individual rivers.
While we may flow in different paths at different
times in our lives, together we make up our family.
Together we are the Amazon river."

Now she could see it. Really see it. How you
could be separate but together. She put her head on

her dad's shoulder. She didn't need a plan or a wish anymore. She would always be best friends with Júlia. Separate but together. And she knew now her family would always be her family. Separate but together. And they would be amazing, just like the Amazon.

Sneak Peek of Another Adventure
Mystery of the Lazy Loggerhead

Chapter One

"What's that?" Sofia Diaz asked.

"*Onde?*" Her Brazilian friend, Júlia Santos, scanned the edge of the beach. She squinted from the early morning rays of the sun. "Where? I don't see anything?"

"It's moving." Sofia kicked her new Havaianas off her tan feet. She made sure to pick them up. They were only the most famous flip flops in the world. She did NOT want to lose them. Sandals safely in hand, she dashed down the beach. The familiar smell of the salt air filled her lungs. The sand kicked up behind her speedy feet.

Sofia stopped a few yards away and pointed. "It's a sea turtle. See her giant head and big jaws? And the reddish-brown and yellow color of her shell? I think she's a loggerhead."

"How do you know she is, how do you say, logger—head?" Júlia asked.

"I know a little about sea turtles." Sofia said. "My grandparents in Florida live near a sea turtle rescue place. I've seen loads of loggerheads there. And she looks the same. She seems slow though."

"Turtles are *all* slow, no?" Júlia giggled. Her brown eyes sparkled. Her light brown skin glowed in the sun.

Sofia spun around and smiled. "Yesssss. But she seems really, really slow. I hope she's not sick."

Júlia shrugged her shoulders. *"Preguiçoso?* Maybe she is lazy?"

"Look!" Sofia pointed at the sand ahead.

Júlia stared at the strange markings in the sand. "They look like small tire tracks."

Sofia kneeled down to inspect the tracks. "They *are* tracks. But not from tires. From a sea turtle."

"Do you think the lazy loggerhead made

them?" Júlia scratched her head.

"Maybe." Sofia looked up and scanned the beach. The lazy loggerhead still crawled slowly along the water's edge.

Júlia knelt down and brushed her hand over the tracks. "Or do you think she led us here?"

"Well, normally, I would say no. But after the troubled toucan . . ." Sofia tilted her head to one side. "Never say never."

Find out what happens to Sofia and Júlia in the Pack-n-Go Girls book, Mystery of the Lazy Loggerhead.

Meet More Pack-n-Go Girls!

Discover Australia with Wendy and Chloe!

Mystery of the Min Min Lights

It's hot. It's windy. It's dusty. It's the Australian outback. Wendy Lee arrives from California. She's lucky to meet Chloe Taylor, who invites Wendy to their sheep station. It sounds like fun except that someone is stealing the sheep. And the thief just might be something as crazy as a UFO.

Discover Austria with Brooke and Eva!

Mystery of the Ballerina Ghost

Nine-year-old Brooke Mason is headed to Austria. She'll stay in Schloss Mueller, an ancient Austrian castle. Eva, the girl who lives in Schloss Mueller, is thrilled to meet Brooke. Unfortunately, the castle's ghost isn't quite so happy. Don't miss the second and third Austria books: *Mystery of the Secret Room* and *Mystery at the Christmas Market*.

Meet More Pack-n-Go Girls!

Discover Mexico with Izzy and Patti!
Mystery of the Thief in the Night
Izzy's family sails into a quiet lagoon in Mexico and drops their anchor. Izzy can't wait to explore the pretty little village, eat yummy tacos, and practice her Spanish. When she meets nine-year-old Patti, Izzy's thrilled. Now she can do all that and have a new friend to play with too. Life is perfect. At least it's perfect until they realize there's a midnight thief on the loose! Don't miss the second Mexico book, *Mystery of the Disappearing Dolphin.*

Discover Thailand with Jess and Nong May!
Mystery of the Golden Temple
Nong May and her family have had a lot of bad luck lately. When nine-year-old Jess arrives in Thailand and accidentally breaks a special family treasure, it seems to only get worse. It turns out the treasure holds a secret that could change things forever!

What to Know Before You Go!

Where is Brazil?

Brazil is the largest country in South America. North of Brazil
is Venezuela and the small countries of Guyana, Suriname,
and French Guiana. West of Brazil you can find Bolivia, Peru,
and Colombia. South of Brazil are Paraguay, Uruguay, and
Argentina. The Atlantic Ocean borders the east side of Brazil.
The shoreline is a whopping 4,655 miles long!

Facts About Brazil

Official Name: Federative Republic of Brazil

Capital: From 1763 to 1960, Rio de Janeiro was the capital of Brazil. Many people wanted to move the capital to a more central location. So they created Brasília. Brasília is a planned city designed in the shape of an airplane.

Currency: Real

Government: Brazil was inhabited by tribal nations before it was discovered by the Portuguese from Portugal in 1500. It was a Portuguese colony until 1808. Then it became a kingdom of the United Kingdom of Portugal, Brazil and the Algarves. In 1822, Brazil became the independent Empire of Brazil. It is now a democratic federative republic.

Language: Portuguese

Population: Brazil is the world's fifth largest country in both its population and its size. As of 2015, its population was over 204 million people.

Traveling in Brazil

When you travel to Brazil, you will get a warm welcome from the people there. They love kids! They also love to have fun. Sometimes the fun can make things pretty loud. You will also need to remember to take your time. Things may not move as quickly as in some other countries, but that's just fine. You are there to have fun, right? Before you go, make sure you have a tourist visa so you can get into the country.

What to Expect for Weather

Most people think Brazil is hot and tropical everywhere. But it's a large country, and different regions of Brazil have different weather. Some places in the mountains even get snow! In Manuas, it is said that there are two seasons: 1) hot and wet and 2) hot and humid. During the summer months of December through March, the almost daily rain cools it down to the mid 70's and 80's. It doesn't always rain in the rainforest, though. During the winter months of June through October, it is drier, but the temperature creeps up. June is the best time to visit the Amazon. The forests are still flooded, the rain has slowed down, and it's still a little cooler.

Brazilian Food

Like the weather, the food in Brazil varies a lot by region. One of the most typical dishes is *feijoada*. This is a black bean stew. It comes with pork, rice, greens, orange chunks, and *farofa*, a dish of toasted flour with bacon, onions, and butter. In Manaus, however, you might be served *tacacá*. This is a soup made with *tucupi*, a root that is actually poisonous before it gets cooked! One thing that you are certain to find in Brazil is coffee. Brazil is the largest coffee producer in the world.

Recipe for Brigadeiro

Ingredients *(If you make this recipe, be sure to get an adult to help you.)*

1 can sweetened condensed milk
1 tablespoon of butter
3 tablespoons of cocoa (use Nesquik for the most authentic flavor)
Sprinkles (chocolate and/or rainbow)

1. Mix the first three ingredients together in a sauce pan.
2. Cook on medium heat until it thickens.
3. Allow it to cool to room temperature.
4. This is where it gets fun! Butter your hands. Yup, butter them! Form the chocolate mixture into 1-inch balls.
5. Roll each ball in the sprinkles.
6. Bite into the yummy chocolate goodness of Brazil.

Say It in Portuguese!

English	Portuguese	Portuguese Pronunciation
Hello	Ola	Oh-LAH
Good morning/day	Bom dia	Bhon DEE-ah
Good afternoon	Boa tarde	BOH-ah TAHR-deh
Good night	Boa noite	BOH-ah NOY-teh
Hi	Oi!	OH-ee
Goodbye	Adeus	Ah-DEH-oosh
Bye	Tchau	Chow
Please	Por favor	Poor fah-VOHR
Thank you	Obrigado/Obrigada	Oh-bree-GAH-doh/dah
Nothing	Nada	NAH-da
Yes/No	Sim/Não	Seen/Now
I don't know	Não sei	Now say
My name is . . .	Meu nome é . . .	MEH-ooh NOH-meh eh
Nice to meet you	Prazer em conhecé-la/lo	Pra-ZAIR eh con-YO-seh-la/lo
Mrs.	Senhora	SENN-yoh-dah
Mr.	Senhor	SEEN-yoh
Let's go!	Vamos!	VA-mos
Cool	Legal	Lay-gah-oo
Geeez!	Uf!	Oof

English	Portuguese	Portuguese Pronunciation
Silence	Silêncio	Seh-LEN-see-oh
Shhhh!	Psui!	PSS-ioo
Don't worry	Não se preocupe	Now seh Pray-o-COO-pe
Yay!	Oba!	OH-bah
Stop!	Pare!	PAH-reh
Great!	Bravo!	BRA-voh
Good	Bem	Behn
Trust me	Confie em mim	CON-fee eh min
0	Zero	ZEH-roo
1	Um/Uma	Oon/Ooma
2	Dois/Duas	Doysh/Doo-ahsh
3	Três	Trehyesh
4	Quatro	KWAH-troo
5	Cinco	SEEN-koo
6	Seis	Saysh
7	Sete	SEH-chee
8	Oito	OY-too
9	Nove	NOH-vee
10	Dez	Daysh

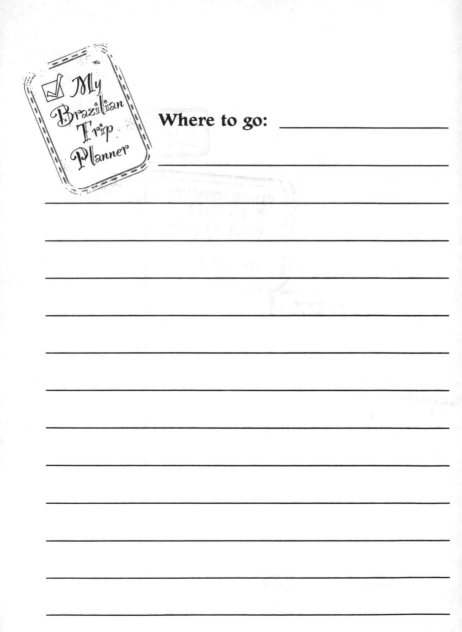

My Brazilian Trip Planner

Where to go: _____

_____

What to do: _____

My Brazilian Trip Planner

_____

_____

_____

_____

_____

_____

_____

_____

_____

_____

_____

_____

_____

_____

_____

_____

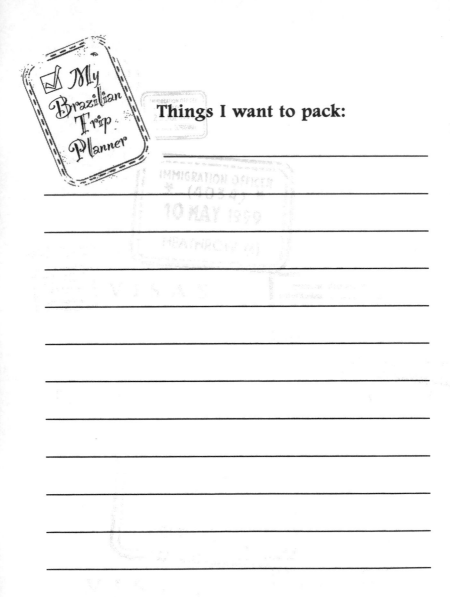

Things I want to pack:

_____

_____

_____

_____

_____

_____

_____

_____

_____

_____

_____

_____

_____

Friends to send postcards to:

_____

_____

_____

_____

_____

_____

_____

_____

_____

_____

_____

_____

Thank you to the following Pack-n-Go Girls:

Anna Allen

Maia Caprice

The Christensens

Addie Cleckler

Keira Clotfelter

Kate Ehrhardt

Beth Ehrhardt

Kate Falender

Tana Hackman

Elizabeth Haddon

Audrey Barineau Mauricio

Reilly O'Boyle

Abby Rice

Faith Sheeks

Klaire Thompson

Sarah Travis

Addison Turner

Serenity Turnquist-McClendon

Leanna Wright

Thank you also to Brynn Barineau, Keri Caprice, Marjorie & Francis Ehrhardt, John & Marilyn Ehrhardt, Joe & Sue Ehrhardt, Lotta Falender, Gregg Friesen, Gerry Jurrens, Charles McClendon, Ashley Rice, Jeannie Sheeks, Lolly Van Teylingen, and all of our Kickstarter supporters.

And a special thanks to my Pack-n-Go Girls co-founder, Janelle Diller, and our husbands, Steve Diller and Rich Travis, who have been along with us on this adventure.

 **Lisa Travis** has always dreamed of faraway places. Her childhood days of exploring old National Geographic magazines in her attic led her to the world beyond. She studied in Germany, traveled the USA in a Volkswagen camper, and lived and worked in South Korea. She currently finds ways to pack and go by designing global leadership programs. Her experiences around the world inspired her to write Pack-n-Go Girls stories that deliver positive messages around independence, adventure, and global awareness. Lisa lives, bikes, and skis in Colorado with her husband, two kids, and two dogs.

Adam Turner has been working as a freelance illustrator since 1987. He has illustrated coloring books, puzzle books, magazine articles, game packaging, and children's books. He's loved to draw ever since he picked up his first pencil as a toddler. Instead of doing the usual two-year-old thing of chewing on it or poking his eye out  with it, he actually put it on paper and thus began the journey. Adam also loves to travel and has had some crazy adventures. He's swum with crocodiles in the Zambezi, jumped out of a perfectly good airplane, and even fished for piranha in the Amazon. It's a good thing drawing relaxes his nerves! Adam lives in Arizona with his wife and their daughter.

Pack-n-Go Girls Online

Dying to know when the next Pack-n-Go Girls book will be out? Want to learn more Portuguese? Trying to figure out what to pack for your next trip? Looking for cool family travel tips? Interested in some fun learning activities about Brazil to use at home or at school while you are reading *Mystery of the Troubled Toucan*?

- Check out our website:
  www.packngogirls.com
- Follow us on Twitter:
  @packngogirls
- Like us on Facebook:
  facebook.com/packngogirls
- Follow us on Instagram:
  packngogirlsadventures
- Discover great ideas on Pinterest:
  Pack-n-Go Girls

CPSIA information can be obtained
at www.ICGtesting.com
Printed in the USA
LVOW10s0017261017
553730LV00012BB/820/P